Tales of
Little Brown Mouse

Alison Uttley was born in Derbyshire and at first educated at a tiny village school. She went to Manchester University, graduating in physics, and then spent a year at Cambridge where she transferred her enthusiasm from science to literature.

When her husband died, leaving her with a little son, she began to write books on country life and animals, incorporating in them many of the tales she had already told to children. Her first stories were written in the 1930s and these well loved tales are now known worldwide.

Alison Uttley was a gifted storyteller with admirers all over the world. She died in 1976 at the age of ninety-one.

Nick
from
Grandpa
1988

Also by Alison Uttley
in Piccolo

Tales of Little Grey Rabbit

Alison Uttley

Tales of
Little Brown Mouse

Illustrated by Faith Jaques

Piccolo Books
in association with Heinemann

First published 1984 by William Heinemann Ltd
This Piccolo edition published 1986 by Pan Books Ltd,
Cavaye Place, London SW10 9PG
in association with William Heinemann Ltd

Text © Alison Uttley Literary Property Trust 1984
Illustrations © Faith Jaques 1984
ISBN 0 330 29243 9
10 9 8 7 6 5 4 3 2 1

Printed and bound in Great Britain by
Cox & Wyman Ltd, Reading

Contents

Snug and Serena
Meet a Queen

Down the lane, sheltered by a wild rose bush, is a little house, hidden in the bank. It is so small you would not notice it unless you stooped and lifted the ferns and grasses, and moved away the curving rose sprays. You might hear the humming and singing and soft laughter if you stood 'as still as a mouse'.

The woodland animals know this place very well. They call it the Rose and Crown, and here they come for their tastes of cowslip wine and dandelion tea.

Over the door hangs the wooden sign, with a picture of a tiny rose and a crown. You might easily mistake it for an autumn leaf dangling from a twig.

There is a porch of twisted rose briars, and in it, on fine days, sit little fieldmice.

They drink from acorn mugs and they smoke clay pipes packed with mouse-baccy, which is wild thyme. The curls of blue smoke float up in the branches of the rose bush and make a sweet smell.

Behind the cosy kitchen and dainty parlour are three or four tiny bedrooms, and store rooms and

cellars, down long winding passages which go deep
into the bank. In the store rooms are heaps of wheat
and barley, the gleanings of the cornfields, and acorns,
beech-mast and cob-nuts.

One bedroom with a goose-feather bed and a peg
for a best jacket belongs to little Snug. It is always
untidy. The blue jacket is seldom on its peg.

Next to it is the bedroom of Serena, his sister. There
is a white bed of hollywood, polished like ivory, and a
peg for the Sunday frock of white silk, and a cupboard
for Serena's treasures. It is a neat room with a rug of
thistledown and a rocking-chair.

Snug and Serena play all day in the bank near their
home. They hide in the long grasses, they run down
the shady paths among violets and primroses, they

suck honey from the cowslip's bell. When it rains they carry violet leaves for umbrellas, and they laugh at the raindrops.

One day Mrs Mouse was very busy. She was expecting a visitor, and there were cakes to be made, and corn to bake.

'Come along, Snug and Serena. Give me a hand,' she called from the doorway, and she rang a harebell to summon her children. They were up a tree, staring at the beetles and ladybirds down below in the lane. When they heard the tinkle of the bell they dropped to the ground.

Snug came running indoors, with his little blue jacket flapping. He tossed his red cap to the mice in the porch. Serena came tumbling after in her yellow skirt.

'Who's coming, mother?' they panted.

'I don't rightly know, childer,' replied Mrs Mouse who was frying the bacon rinds over a bright fire. 'I'm sure it's fine company for Robin the Postman brought a letter and only grand folk write on silver-birch bark with a gold crest on the back.'

Serena picked up the folded scrap of silver birch and Mrs Mouse read it again. 'ʏᴘᴇᴄᴛ ᴍᴇ ᴛᴏ ᴅɪɴ.'

'It may be Mr Mole or Mr Frog,' said Serena.

'Or a Harvest Mouse,' said Snug.

'Or Tom Hedgehog,' said Serena.

'I think it's royalty,' said Mrs Mouse, and she nodded her head and went back to her cooking.

'Fill the tea-kettle, Snug,' she cried, and Snug ran out to the stream with the tin kettle.

'Get me a mouse-lettuce, Serena,' she commanded, and Serena darted to the lane and picked the delicate sour leaves of the wood-sorrel.

'I want violet petals for a salad, Serena,' called her mother, 'and an egg for an omelette.'

Good little Serena picked the violets and then she climbed a hawthorn tree to a nest where a chaffinch sat.

'Have you a spare egg, please?' asked Serena. 'Mother's expecting company and she wants an egg.'

'Certainly not,' cried the indignant chaffinch, and she puffed out her feathers and pecked at Serena, till the little mouse nearly fell backwards in a fright.

Every nest she visited it was the same. Nobody could spare an egg for Mrs Mouse's omelette. Serena had just decided that she must go to the farmyard and trundle an egg home, when the turtle-dove took pity on her.

'I'll leave an egg at your door,' said the dove, and the gentle bird flew down and laid an egg on the moss near the front door of the Rose and Crown.

'Oh, thank you, thank you very much,' cried Mrs Mouse.

Serena stayed a moment to pick the sweet hawthorn leaves, which country children call 'bread-and-cheese'.

'Serena. Our Serena,' called a piping voice, and little Snug came to join her.

'I'm going to sit here and look out for the company. Father says so. I'm the look-out mouse,' said he, proudly, and he stuck a little telescope of straw to his eye and peered all round.

'I wonder who it will be,' said Serena. 'I am glad we are going to have company.'

'They won't want you. Company sits all alone, very grand,' said Snug.

Serena ran home with her leaves and flowers, and Mrs Mouse chopped them and put them in the salad.

The bread-and-cheese went in one walnut shell, may-buds and mouse-lettuce in another, primroses and violets in a third. Serena whisked the dove's egg ready for the omelette.

Mr Mouse came puffing up from the cellars carrying bottles, cobwebbed and dirty.

'Must get all ready,' said he. 'Honeymead's a likely drink.'

He rubbed the bottles clean on his green baize apron and set them on the floor to warm in the sunshine.

'Mester Mouse, who are you expecting of?' called Timothy Snout, one of the ancients in the porch. 'Is it King and Queen? If so I mun be off to tidy myself.'

'I think it's royalty, Timothy Snout,' said William Mouse, drawing out the corks with a pop.

'Bring me a mug of dandelion, if you please, to drink their healths,' cried another mouse, Samuel Furze. He lived in the gorse bush, and he was always thirsty.

'Mester Mouse. Bring me a jug of that honeymead,' called a third, old John Barleycorn.

Suddenly there was a shout from the hawthorn tree.

'Here they are! Here they are! Hundreds of 'em.'

12

Snug slipped down, catching his trousers on a thorn and hanging there for a minute as he shouted, 'Hundreds and hundreds.'

Then the trousers split and he fell among the startled mice near the door of the Rose and Crown.

'I've seen them,' said Snug, excitedly. 'There's a glass coach rolling over the field with a crowd flying round it. Hundreds of 'em. It's the littlest coach you ever saw. It's got a gold crown on the top, like our sign.'

'I can hear them, all singing and humming,' said Serena, her hand to her pointed furry ear.

'It's the Queen Bee,' cried Mrs Mouse. 'It must be the Queen Bee swarming. You childer brush your hair and wash your hands while I tidy myself. Queens are very particular.'

Serena and Snug sleeked their fur with tiny teasel brushes, and washed their hands and faces in the little bowl on the table.

'William, put on your best jacket, and get ready to receive the Queen,' continued Mrs Mouse. 'All of you must bow and curtsey. Remember your manners.'

'The Queen Bee,' said Mr Mouse slowly, and he put down the tankards he was carrying and untied his apron, and brushed his whiskers and head. Then he slipped on his best ruby coat.

'Deary me! I hope she isn't going to be a nuisance and bring her swarm here. We've no room for a swarm of bees. No room at all. What will happen to the Rose and Crown if all that crowd comes in? There'd be no room for us. They'll sting us and drive us away. Deary me.'

'Put some mugs of honeymead on the bank and maybe she won't come in,' advised Timothy Snout.

'Set some honey-cakes on the grass, and shut the door,' said Samuel Furze.

'Beat your drum and bang your fire-irons,' said old John Barleycorn.

But before anyone could prepare, the humming grew very near, and a dark cloud of bees hovered outside the inn. From her glass coach the Queen Bee looked out.

'Stop,' she commanded. 'Here is the famous Rose and Crown. We will live here. It's a good inn with food and rooms ready.'

Mrs Mouse came forward with a low curtsey, and Mr Mouse gave a nervous bow. Snug and Serena bobbed.

'Good day, Your Majesty,' said they.

'A swarm of bees in May
    Is worth a load of hay,'
piped old Timothy Snout.

'Yes, we are a valuable swarm,' said the Queen,
proudly. 'We will honour you with our company. We
will take the Rose and Crown – lock, stock and barrel,
wine, mead and barley-brew.'

Mr Mouse turned pale. He carried out a bowl of
honey wine and the Queen dipped her own silver cup
into it. She drank and then threw away the little cup.
All the bees hovered about, drinking the honey wine
from the bottles and glasses.

15

'Landlord,' said the Queen. 'We shall want the whole of your inn, and food and wine.'

'Please Your Majesty, I don't think it is big enough to hold all of you,' stammered poor Mr Mouse.

'Not big enough for my bees and you, but you must move out,' said the Queen, coldly, and she stepped from the coach and came towards the door with the great crowd buzzing behind her.

Little Serena kept close to her mother and Mrs Mouse stood with her back to the door ready to defend her home. Then young Snug came forward.

'Please, Your Majesty,' said he, bowing. 'I know of a beautiful palace, white as snow, sweet as honey, with lots of room in it, and a fine doorway, and a garden of flowers.'

Everyone stared at Snug.

'Where is this palace?' asked the Queen Bee.

'At the farmhouse,' said Snug, simply. 'It's a new hive all ready for a swarm of bees. There's a stream near, and a clover field. You'll be welcome as a load of hay there, Your Majesty.'

'A clover field! A new hive! To the farm we will go,' said the Queen, and she climbed into the coach. 'If ever you want some honeycomb, knock at the palace door and one of my workers will give you some.'

She waved her hand and the swarm rose high in the air with the coach in the middle. With a loud humming they flew away, over the field to the farm and the new hive.

Mrs Mouse trembled with relief, and Mr Mouse wiped his face with his large red handkerchief.

'Well done, Snug! You've saved the Rose and Crown,' said he. 'I thought we should have to go.'

'How did you know about the hive?' asked Mrs Mouse.

'Oh, I saw it one day, when I was exploring,' said Snug.

'Crowns of gold are all right, but I like humble folk in leather leggings and jackets and scarves,' said Mr Mouse.

Little Serena came running up. 'Here's the silver cup the Queen threw away,' she cried, holding a tiny cup like a flower.

'And here's a gold slipper she lost,' added Snug, and he picked up the slipper from the grass.

'We'll keep them safe in memory of royalty's visit,' said Mrs Mouse, and she put them in Serena's cupboard among her treasures.

'Another visitor's a-coming up the lane,' called Timothy Snout. 'It's the Toad, creeping along, slow as a snail.'

Up the lane waddled a Toad, with striped waistcoat, and yellow buttons and buff breeches. He hobbled along; he stared at the sky; he looked at the grass; he drank from a stream – he certainly took his time.

'Good day, Timothy. Good day, Samuel. Good day, John Barleycorn,' he greeted the mice, and he rapped at the inn door with the knob of his stick.

'Anyone at home?' he asked.

'Oh come in, Mr Toad,' cried Mrs Mouse, smoothing her apron.

'Come in, sir,' said Mr Mouse, throwing wide the door.

The Toad rubbed his damp feet on the doormat for a long time, and then he put his stick in the corner of the room. He sat down in the armchair Mr Mouse brought forward for him, and he looked round with a broad smile.

'Did you get my letter, Ma'am?' he asked.

'Was it yours?' cried Mr Mouse. 'We thought it was royalty, and royalty has just been here.'

'Royalty didn't eat my dinner, I hope,' said the Toad.

'No. The Queen Bee had a sip of honey wine but no more,' said Mrs Mouse, firmly. 'No more, although she wanted a lot.'

'There was a gold crest on the letter,' said Mr Mouse.

'Oh that! Yes, it was a bit of sunshine I caught in my fishing-net,' explained Mr Toad, airily. 'I stuck it on the letter to smarten it up.'

'It made us all hurry, Mr Toad,' said Mrs Mouse, smiling. 'Now I'll make the omelette, sir.' She whipped up the egg again and added the herbs.

Two little mice came out to stare at the Toad. They liked his big face, his bright eyes and humped head. They liked his webbed feet and his creased coat and bulky pockets.

'Now you two children,' said Mr Toad. 'What shall it be? A lollipop? A story? A present?'

'Whatever you like, Mr Toad,' stammered Serena.

'A lollipop first,' said Snug.

The Toad put his hand in his deep pocket and brought out some striped sweets wrapped in a kingcup leaf. From another pocket he brought a paintbox rolled up in silvery waterleaves, and from yet another came a willow cricket bat about two inches long, and lastly he fished out a beautiful little fiddle, called a jig, which he used for dances.

'Oh, thank you. Thank you, Mr Toad,' cried the young mice, and they sat on the floor with the lollipops between them, while the smiling old Toad told them a fairy story.

'Once upon a time,' he began in his croaking voice. 'Once upon a time, there lived in the depths of a deep, deep well, a Royal Toad.'

'Dinner's ready,' called Mrs Mouse.

She had set the table with her clean cloth, and put on it her best rose-bud china, and wooden spoons and blue mugs and green glasses.

'Dinner's ready, please sir,' announced Mrs Mouse again and she rang the little harebell.

'You must all join me,' said Mr Toad, looking up. 'I don't want to dine alone. Everyone must come.'

'You won't go home, will you, Mr Toad?' asked Serena, pulling her chair close to Mr Toad's.

'Have you a spare room, Mrs Mouse?' asked the Toad, glancing towards her.

'A beautiful room, with running water for washing your feet,' said Mrs Mouse, proudly. 'There's a feather bed and clean sheets.'

'Then I'll stay the night, Mrs Mouse,' said he. 'I wanted to visit the Rose and Crown, and sample Mrs Mouse's cooking. Tomorrow I shall go on my way to my castle, but tonight I will stay with your pleasant company.'

After dinner the Toad told them another tale, and played his fiddle to the two little mice. Mrs Mouse fetched her knitting and Mr Mouse smoked his pipe.

When dusk fell and the first star appeared in the sky, the Toad asked for his candle. They took him to the spare room where a trickle of water flowed, and he said good night.

'This is just my kind of bedroom,' said he, dipping his toes in the stream.

Snug and Serena could hear him singing as they lay

in their own small beds and the words came floating
down the underground passage.

> 'Oh, the Rose and the Crown,
> With green leaves and brown.
> In summer and spring
> The turtle-doves sing,
> At the Rose and the Crown.
> It is fit for a king,
> Is the Rose and the Crown.'

'Is he royal?' whispered Serena.
'Is he a king?' asked Snug.

The Flower Show

This is the story of how Snug and Serena went to a flower show. It was not a mouse flower show in the hedge bank where the wild thyme grows, but a grown-up show in a tent to which fieldmice are not invited.

One day Snug and Serena were playing hide-and-seek in a hollow piece of oak. It was a small, curly branch, silvery with lichen, and inside was a hole lined with moss, leading to a tiny room. It was so narrow only two small mice could enter.

'This is a secret house where we can hide,' said little Serena. 'We can come here and nobody will ever find us.'

'Why, there's a cupboard in here,' cried Snug. 'Let's fill it with honey and then we can stay as long as we like.'

Off they ran to the wild bees' honeycomb in a tree, and they broke off a scrap and carried it to the cupboard. They were just going out to find more when they heard footsteps coming down the lane. They knew it was a human coming along.

They stayed very still, but their oak branch was lifted up.

'This is just what I want for my flower decoration,' said a voice.

Snug and Serena clung to one another.

'Are you frightened, Serena?' whispered Snug.

'No,' laughed Serena. 'Are you?'

'Not at all,' said Snug, boldly. 'It's an adventure. Let's see what happens.'

The lady took the hollow piece of wood to her cottage in the village. When Snug heard the church bell he knew where he was.

They tumbled about in the hollow, but they never made a squeak even when a cat came sniffing round.

'Go away, Puss! Go away!' said Miss Smith sternly. 'Don't dare to touch my lovely tree.'

The branch was fixed in a bowl of water. Hart's-tongue ferns were planted by it, and some flowers, with a bunch of green grapes to hang down the side.

'Very nice indeed,' said the voices, and everybody admired the lichened tree.

'The little mossy hole is most attractive,' said someone and a finger was poked inside the hollow. Snug and Serena drew back.

'Shall I bite it?' whispered Snug, but Serena nudged him to be quiet.

'Tomorrow morning I shall take this to the flower show and I am sure I shall get a prize,' said Miss Smith.

'Did you hear that?' asked Snug. 'A flower show. I always wanted to see a real flower show.'

'There will be lots to eat,' said Serena eagerly. 'I'm getting so hungry, Snug. I'm glad we have this honey in the cupboard.'

They had supper and then they slept soundly. At dawn a ray of sunshine came through the tiny mossy doorway and they opened their eyes.

'Where am I?' asked Serena, sleepily.

They both peeped timidly out but the cat was not there and the room was empty. They climbed down the branch, leapt over the water, and walked on the table. There were delicious morsels of food lying ready for them, bits of cheese, and some butter. The two wrinkled their noses with pleasure and ate a good breakfast. They were dancing about when they heard a sound, and they scurried back across the water into the hollow branch.

'Oh dear, I've lost a slipper,' murmured Serena, holding out her foot. 'It fell off when I ran so fast.'

Miss Smith came again to admire her bowl. She rearranged it, and then she carried it with its tree and fruit and flowers to the flower show. It was placed on a table among several other vases and bowls of flowers.

The tent was closed, and it was quiet. The little mice peered out.

They poked out their heads and their little paws, and then they stepped warily down the crooked silver oak.

They saw dishes of ripe plums, blue as night, and yellow pears and red apples. They cried out in surprise at the giant onions, tied in top-knots, and the long scarlet runners.

'Look! Look!' cried Serena, picking up her skirt and dancing on bare toes. They tasted the raspberries and plums, with little nibbles, and then they went across the tables to look at the strange flowers. There were roses like silk cushions upon which they could sit, and snapdragons which snapped their yellow mouths at them, and stocks which held parcels of perfume, and mignonette which carried little green purses full of mouse-money on their stalks.

Every flower nodded its head to the two little mice who fluttered like butterflies over the tables.

They came to the jam jars which the school children had filled with collections of wild flowers. There were harebells to ring, and willow-herb to climb like a ladder, and purple cushions of scabious which Mrs Mouse used for her pincushions, and tansy which she put in a pie, and scented meadow-sweet. 'All the flowers we know are here,' said Serena. 'Even wild thyme and marjoram.'

'Useful for soup,' said Snug, wisely.

'We'll give them all the first prizes,' said Serena.

'FIRST PRIZE' she wrote on a label in mouse-language.

The women of the village had made some little rock gardens in plates and dishes with sand for paths, and water, and a few plants growing among the rocks. When Snug and Serena found them, they ran along the paths, washed their faces in the pools and leapt from the rocks.

'Gardens for us,' laughed Serena. 'They must have guessed we were coming.'

They dragged some corn-stalks from a vase, and wove a little house from the straw, like a harvest mouse's nest. They put wheat ears at the top in a tassel. Then they placed the round straw house in one of the gardens, where it was like a fairy cot.

'Now let us make a basket from the grasses,' said Serena. 'Let's show them what we can do.'

They plaited a couple of grass baskets and filled them with flower heads and little berries.

They nibbled some rose petals to make lace mats and put them among the needlework.

'Humans do make big stitches,' observed Serena, looking at the white stitches in a cloth. 'They should see our mother's sewing.'

She began to sing:

> 'A mouse does the sewing
> With stitches so small
> You scarcely can see them
> At all, at all.
>
> A mouse does the mending,
> And no one can see,
> The patch or the darn,
> So wee, so wee.'

'Quiet!' hissed Snug. 'You'll wake the people.'

'Let us make our own bowls of flowers,' said Serena, hopping and skipping joyfully.

'Here's a flower-pot,' said Snug.

He held up a silver thimble which had been left on the table.

They filled the thimble with a bouquet of the tiniest flowers. They put in miniature roses and florets of meadow-sweet, a daisy, sprigs of grasses, and bells, so that it was the prettiest little pot of flowers ever seen.

'I'm getting hungry,' said Serena. 'Find some food, Snug.'

They darted along the tables to the cookery exhibits. Cream cheeses, golden tarts, iced cakes, scones and pastry were arranged on plates ready for the judging.

'I do like a flower show like this,' said Snug, helping himself to the iced sponge cake. 'This is worth first prize.'

'All first prizes,' agreed Serena, dreamily, as she nibbled each cake.

There was a rumble of voices, the tent opened, and the judges entered.

'No time to get back,' muttered Snug. 'Run, Serena.' They scuttered down the table legs to the floor; they ran through the thick grass and escaped under the edge of the tent.

A voice cried out, 'Look! Look at these tiny vases! Flowers in a thimble! It's a fairy's work!'

Then another voice exclaimed. 'This straw house is remarkably well made. This is a gem of a garden, with little baskets of flowers.'

Somebody said, 'This flower arrangement with the lichened branch is clever, but what is sticking out of the mossy hole? A little red shoe? A yellow handkerchief?

'There!' cried Snug. 'You've gone and lost your other slipper!'

'And you've lost your hanky!' retorted Serena.

'Let us get away at once,' said Snug, so they did not hear the cries when the judges saw the cakes each with two little nibbles and two little bites.

'I know the way home,' said Snug. 'Follow me.'

They went along the invisible footpaths to the field.

They crossed the field and entered the lane and at last they saw the chimneys of the Rose and Crown, hidden under the rose tree. There was the dear mossy roof and the washing hanging out in the garden.

Mrs Mouse came running to meet them, crying, 'Oh, children, where have you been?'

'Serena and Snug,' scolded Mr Mouse, rushing up from the cellar. 'You are very naughty indeed.'

'We've been to a flower show down by the church,' boasted Snug.

'We made baskets of flowers and a summer hut,' added Serena.

'And Serena lost her shoes, one in a house and one in the flower show,' said Snug.

'In a house! In a flower show!' Mrs Mouse nearly fainted.

Snug and Serena told their adventures, and the family listened, astonished.

Down in the village the judges were puzzled.

'Mice have been tasting everything – a nibble here, a nibble there, just a bit,' said they.

'Fairies have been here to fill this thimble and to make these baskets of flowers,' said others.

'Is it mice or fairies?' asked a little girl.

'We really don't know,' confessed the judges. 'There was a tiny red slipper and a yellow hanky in that silvery tree, and Miss Smith found another red slipper on her kitchen floor. It is all very mysterious.'

'I think it was Snug and Serena,' said the little girl.

But everyone laughed, for how could she know?

Going to the Fair

One day Snug was trotting along a green track in the field when he saw a straw house under the hedge. It was a caravan made out of wheat-stalks, with a chimney on top, a door at the back, and a handle to pull it along.

At the door sat two harvest mice busily weaving little baskets of straw to hold grain.

Snug hid behind a dandelion, but the mice had seen him.

'I knew your red trousers, young Mousekin,' said Mr Harvest. 'I saw 'em once at the Rose and Crown.'

'As red as corn poppies,' added Mrs Harvest.

'Can't help seeing you,' said Mr Harvest. 'But never mind our jokes. Just take a peep at the caravan.'

Snug ran into the straw house which held many little baskets fitted into one another.

'Do you live here?' he asked.

'No, we live in the cornfield,' said Mrs Harvest. 'We are basket-makers, on the way to the fair.'

'The fair?' echoed Snug. 'Where is it?'

'In the corner of the orchard,' said Mr Harvest. 'Everyone knows about it. You be off home and ask if they've forgotten the May Fair.'

As Snug ran he saw the yellow skirt of his sister Serena fluttering in the bushes like a brimstone butterfly.

'Hello, Serena,' he called. 'Have you heard there's a fair?'

Serena crept out of the gorse.

'A fair?' she cried. 'Oh, let's go! I've never seen a fair.'

When they got home there was a chatter and squeak in the Rose and Crown. A gypsy hedgehog was there, with a basket of clothes-pegs made out of thorns like her own prickles.

'Yes, I'm going to the May Fair,' said she. 'It's in the orchard.'

She picked up her basket and then she stared at Snug.

'We shan't miss seeing you, in your red trousers,' said she. 'You're like a poppy in the corn.'

She laughed and away she went, singing.

'The rude prickly-bob,' pouted Snug. 'I'm not a poppy in the corn.'

'Now, everybody stop talking,' said Mrs Mouse, ringing her harebell for silence. 'We are going to the fair and we must get ready at once.'

'I saw some basket-makers with a yellow caravan under the hedge. They told me,' cried Snug, eagerly.

'Be quiet and do as you're bid,' said Mrs Mouse. 'An unbiddable mouse stays at home. Snug and Serena, wash yourselves.'

Mrs Mouse bustled around making lettuce and egg sandwiches. Serena and Snug washed their faces and brushed their fur. Mr Mouse struggled into his best coat.

The key he hid under a dandelion. Laughing, talking, the four set off down the narrow track at the side of the lane. They kept to the grass where they were safe. The path was worn by many small feet pattering there all day long and sometimes into the night.

They saw a butterfly fast in a spider's web and little Snug unfastened the knots of silken rope and set her free.

'Thank you, Snug,' said the butterfly.

On they went, sipping from the honey-bags of the white dead-nettle, nibbling the sweet hawthorn leaves, biting sour wood-sorrel, blowing at dandelion clocks to find the time.

'Oh, there's the caravan with the basket-makers,' cried Snug, and over the grass trundled the little yellow house, with Mrs Harvest pushing and Mr Harvest pulling it.

'Going to the Fair?' called Mr Mouse, and the harvest mice nodded.

'A hard-working couple, those harvest mice,' said Mr Mouse. 'Good weavers and very knowledgeable about corn.'

Now they could hear the tinkling of flowery bells, the rattle of grasses, the music of a fiddle and a harp of silvery tone.

In the orchard among the flowers of spring, the fair was held. At first the mice walked about, looking at the stalls, admiring the display. There were piles of golden wheat and barley, of dried acorns and cobnuts, which had been stored all the winter and were put out for sale. Brown cakes and sugar sticks were heaped on broad sycamore leaves.

Little animals hurried to and fro, emptying their baskets for the customers to buy and the customers strolled about and met their friends and relations. Hedgehogs stood in one corner, buying clothes-pegs and teazle-brushes from the gypsy.

Mrs Mouse and Serena loitered by a ribbon stall, and they bought some green-striped ribbon-grasses which had come from the garden beyond the wall.

They found a red pincushion and a walnut-shell box. There was a doll, too, made of poppy-petals and Serena bought it for a mouse-penny. Snug begged for a whip and top.

Suddenly, when all were enjoying themselves, a drum sounded, a rabbit's foot thumped the earth, and a trumpet squeaked. It was the alarm for DANGER!

Every little animal dropped to the ground and disappeared, either in the shelter of the wall, or down one of the narrow passages which go underground in fields and lanes and pastures to the safety caverns of the small animals of the wild. With them went Snug and Serena, running as fast as their little legs would carry them, Mrs Mouse panting behind and Mr Mouse following his family.

'What is it, father? A lion?' asked Snug, trembling with excitement.

'Only a hawk, my son,' said Mr Mouse, calmly. 'Always hide when a wind-hover appears. If you don't hide, then be still and it may not see you.'

Ribbons and laces fell to the ground, toys were scattered. The harvest mice had gone into their caravan, the hedgehogs rolled themselves in balls. The animals whispered as they watched the hawk's shadow pass over the ground. Then away flew the keen-eyed bird and the fair went on.

'Oh dear!' sighed Mrs Mouse. 'I can't abide hawks. They are like cats flying up there, with sharp eyes and fierce claws.'

'Why, there's Timothy Snout and Samuel Furze and John Barleycorn,' shouted Mr Mouse, hailing his old friends.

'I've brought my family to see the fair,' he told them, and Mrs Mouse bobbed a curtsey and the three ancient mice bowed to her.

'Join us at dinner,' suggested Mrs Mouse. 'We have enough for everybody. Come and sit with us.'

So they sat on the sunny bank. John Barleycorn brought a few honey cakes from his pocket, and laid them on the grass, and Timothy added a round cheese his wife had made. Then Samuel put out a lardy-cake – and what a feast they had!

Snug and Serena dipped their toes in the stream and fished for minnows with rods made of green rushes. Tim Rabbit came up and played his flute for them to dance.

Little Tom Hedgehog showed Serena how to play darts, and Wat Hare tossed his cowslip ball into her lap for a present.

'Now we'll go and buy some fairings,' said Timothy Snout, and he took his leather purse from his pocket and counted his green pennies.

For Serena he bought a necklace of blue beads, made from the seeds of a rare flower in the garden.

Snug chose a humming-top which played a tune. It had been carved from a nut by a champion carver.

Then Snug wandered off alone, exploring the big orchard. 'There's music somewhere,' he whispered to himself, and, indeed, a queer little air had been tinkling through the fairground.

Behind the bee-hive, hanging from the low bough of an apple-tree was a swing, and near it sat Pin Hedgehog, ragged and rough, played a mouth-organ.

'Can I have a swing?' asked Snug, holding out his penny, and the old scarecrow nodded.

'Be ye careful. Many a mouse gets missed,' said he.

Then away soared the swing, up towards the sky, down to the ground. The wind rushed through Snug's fur and the wide world seemed to be swinging too, as the music of the mouth-organ sang below.

A shadow fell on the grass, the drum beat, the rabbit thumped its foot for DANGER, and the alarm trumpet sounded. Every animal fled to shelter, except little Snug who went on swinging.

'Stop! Stop!' cried the showman, taking cover, but it was too late. Down like a stone fell the hawk, down to the earth, for its eye had caught the gleam of Snug's red trousers. Then with Snug in its claws it rose in the air. It held Snug firmly by his trousers, and it carried him to the church tower where it had its nest.

All the young hawks were waiting for dinner. They put their heads over the edge of the nest and watched their mother.

'There's something special today,' they told each other with shrill cries of hunger.

'Here's little Red Trousers for your dinner,' called the hawk, resting on the ledge of the tower.

'Please, please, please,' squeaked Snug.

'You are not very fat after all,' said the hawk, sternly. 'You are only a morsel among my family.'

The hawk fastened Snug to the iron weather-cock by his trousers and coat, and there he hung, swinging in the wind, while all the young birds cried for him.

Down flew the hawk, circling the valley, seeking more food.

Snug struggled but could not get free.

He dragged one arm from his jacket and then the other. Holding the metal foot of the weather-cock, he slipped his thin legs out of the trousers, which flapped in the wind. He hung by his tail for a moment, while his little coat and trousers ballooned on the weather-cock, just as if he were inside them.

He took one look at the earth far below, he gave a faint cry and then he dived into the air.

He landed, dazed and bruised, on a patch of moss, and he just managed to creep into the shelter of some ferns when the hawk returned.

'Quick! We are hungry!' screamed the little hawks, as the mother went to the weather-cock to seize the empty jacket and trousers.

'Gone! Vanished!' cried the astonished hawk.

Snug lay very still. After a time a ladybird found him and she gave him a spotted cloak to wrap round him. It was so small Snug used it as a handkerchief to dry his tears. A butterfly hovered near, and she gave him a sip of honey to revive him. Two ants brought an oak leaf to cover him. A sunbeam warmed him, and a spider spun a web over his cuts and hurts.

He lay there until it was dusk, when he ventured out. He wandered a long way, lost in the wide countryside, until suddenly he saw the gleam of a tiny light. He crept up, and he tapped on a tiny door.

In the meantime Mr and Mrs Mouse and Serena were hunting everywhere.

The old showman hedgehog told how a hawk, a wind-hover, had carried off the little mouse.

'It was the red trousers, ma'am,' explained Pin Hedgehog. 'Too bright he was, like a poppy in a cornfield.'

Sadly they went home to the Rose and Crown. At night Mrs Mouse put a lighted candle in her window, and Mr Mouse hung a lantern from the porch. He went out to ask all his friends to look for little Snug in field and dell.

'I'll go and hunt for him,' said Mr Toad, who was wandering in the lane.

Off he waddled and first he saw Policeman Owl sailing serenly over the hedge.

'Tawny! Tawny!' he called. 'Have you seen little Snug?'

'Too-whit, too-whoo,' hooted Tawny Owl. 'I saw a pair of red trousers on the weather-cock, but nobody was inside them.'

'Eaten up,' sighed the Toad. 'It's that hawk.' He asked moles, hedgehogs, bit-bats, snails, but nobody had seen little Snug. He trudged across the fields, and over the common. He was just going to turn back when he heard muffled laughter. He stopped. A small shrill voice was singing and he recognized the song.

'Oh, the Rose and the Crown,
With green leaves and brown.
In summer and spring
The turtle-doves sing,
At the Rose and the Crown.
It is fit for a king,
Is the Rose and the Crown.'

'Where is he? Where is the varmint hiding?' cried Toad.

The laughter came from a bunch of straw in the tall wet grasses. A glow-worm light shone in a window.

'Is that you, Snug?' called Toad. The tiny door opened and a flood of light streamed out. Mr and Mrs Harvest and Snug looked down from the straw caravan.

'Oh, Mr Toad,' cried Snug, leaping down the step. 'Come inside. We're having supper.'

'Where have you been, Snug? Do you know your poor father is looking for you and your mother is weeping? Here you are, enjoying yourself. You ought to be ashamed!'

Toad was very indignant.

'Please sir,' interrupted Mr Harvest. 'Please, we found him lost and cold without his trousers and bruised with tumbling from the top of the church steeple. So we bandaged him and gave him a good feed and now he is singing to us.'

'Yes, Mr Toad,' said Snug, showing his bandages.

'Thank you very much,' cried Toad, shaking hands

with the harvest mice. 'Thank you, and if you come to the Rose and Crown, Mr William Mouse will thank you himself.'

The harvest mice said it had been a pleasure to entertain such a knowing little mouse as Snug.

'Now come along with me,' said Mr Toad, taking Snug's arm, and they crept slowly home.

What a greeting there was when they arrived! What drinks of hot milk with a sprig of lemon balm to keep out the cold!

'Oh, my darling Snug!' cried Mrs Mouse, throwing her arms round little Snug, so that he nearly choked. 'I am so glad to see you safe and sound! Never mind your old trousers. I will make a new pair tomorrow.'

'Not red trousers,' implored Snug. 'I don't want to be a poppy in the corn. I want to be invisible like the harvest mice.'

'Well, we'll see,' promised Mrs Mouse, smiling.

She bathed Snug's bruises in sweet balsam from her herb cupboard, and put on ointment of self-heal. The next day the little mouse was completely cured with never an ache or pain.

She stitched and stitched with her tiny needle and made a pair of brown trousers and a shadowy blue coat just like the smoke from a wood fire.

At night Snug skipped out to dance in the moonlight and Serena danced with him.

'Hello, Snug,' whispered the harvest mice, and Snug saw their straw caravan drawn up under a foxglove.

'Here we are,' said Mrs Harvest shyly.

'Welcome! Welcome!' shouted Mr Mouse, as they walked into the house. 'Come and sit by my fire. Meet all my friends. Here's Mr Toad, and Samuel Furze and John Barleycorn, and Timothy, and my wife, all wishing to thank you.'

So they had supper, and the young ones sat on the floor, for there wasn't room at the table. They sang merry songs, and toasted Mr and Mrs Harvest.

At last they all went to bed – the Toad in the guest room, the three old mice on the kitchen floor, and the harvest mice in the caravan. Snug begged to sleep there too, and he lay on a heap of straw, in the tiny yellow house.

The next day the caravan went away, filled with good food.

'We'll see you again, after the harvest,' called the little couple. 'Goodbye, Mr Mouse, and Mrs Mouse. Goodbye, Serena and Snug. Goodbye, Mr Toad.'

They trundled the caravan down the lane among the ferns and buttercups, and soon it was out of sight.

Snug and the Silver Spoon

One day Snug thought he would go a-fishing like his father.

'Please, father, will you lend me your fishing-rod?' he asked.

'Certainly not,' answered Mr Mouse, who was busy boiling dandelions to make a yellow syrup. 'Come along, Snug! Make yourself useful! A fat little mouse like you ought to be able to stir my syrup.'

Snug took the long wooden spoon and stirred the mixture. Swirls of steam rose and he sniffed and sniffed. It was very nice!

'A pinch of ginger, and a piece of honeycomb, Snug,' said Mr Mouse, and he sprinkled the ginger and added the honey to the pan.

'And now, what did you say about fishing?' he asked.

'Please will you lend me your fishing-rod. I'm going a-fishing,' said Snug, boldly.

'Not with my rod, but you can make your own,' said Mr Mouse firmly. 'I'll show you while the dandelion syrup cools.'

51

He lifted the brass pan to the ground and then he went out with Snug to the field.

'Get me some of those rushes,' said Mr Mouse.

Snug ran to gather the long green rushes. Mr Mouse tied a wild strawberry to the tip for the bait. He plaited the other end with bindweed to make a handle.

'Now you can fish with this, and if you're lucky you *may* catch a fish,' said he.

Little Serena came tumbling through the hedge, eager to see what was happening.

'And what do you want, Miss Serena?' asked her father.

'Please, a fishing-rod too. I want to go a-fishing,' said Serena.

So Mr Mouse made another fishing-rod, and this time he tied a wild raspberry on the tip for the bait.

'Now you two can go a-fishing and don't you fall in. Take care of yourselves, and mind the Stoats and Weasels.'

'Yes, Father,' said Snug and Serena, obediently.

'And you'd better make a basket to carry home your catch. Make a big basket,' said Mr Mouse.

'Oh yes,' said Snug. 'I 'specks we shall catch a whale.'

Mr Mouse returned to the Rose and Crown to finish his dandelion syrup, and the two little mice ran about gathering grasses to weave into a basket. They made a long-shaped basket, because fish are long, and they wove a cover to keep the fish from leaping out. So at last they went to the river.

Either the bait was too tasty, or the mice were not very clever, but every time they dipped the rods into the water a fish nibbled first at the strawberry, then at the raspberry.

'Very nice strawberries grow up there,' said one little fish to another. 'Snug and Serena are giving a party.'

'Nice raspberries too,' said the other fish.

'I wish something would happen,' said Serena, slowly, as she watched the ripples spreading in circles and the fish popping up their heads. 'I don't think I like fishing as much as I expected.'

A ripple spread across the water as a boat approached. The fishes hurried away, but Snug and Serena called as they recognized Mr Toad. His boat was a water-lily pad, and he rowed with a pair of slender oars.

He looked rather unhappy, and this was strange for Mr Toad was a calm and comfortable animal.

'It isn't on water and it isn't on land,' he murmured, staring at Snug and Serena as if he had forgotten them.

'Dear Mr Toad. Come and see us catching fish,' said Serena.

'It isn't in the mud and it isn't in the rushes,' said Mr Toad, miserably.

'What have you lost, Mr Toad?' asked Serena.

Then the Toad saw his friends.

'Snug and Serena! Oh dear me! I wonder if you can help,' said he. 'I've lost my silver spoon.'

'What is it like?' asked Snug.

'It is a very beautiful spoon, given to my ancestors.

It has wavy lines like feathers round the handle, and it is small enough for a toad to use for his dinner. It was made by the royal silversmith for the little princess, but it was so tiny she gave it to a pet toad. He lived in her garden, and he ate from a little bowl of food she prepared for him every day. So she gave him this tiny silver spoon. To her surprise he took it in his hand and lapped up his soup. The king and the courtiers came to see the marvel, but this frightened the toad so much he waddled away with the spoon and never returned.'

'Oh, Mr Toad,' murmured Serena. 'Oh!'

'He was my great-great-great-grandfather, Sir Timothy Toad,' continued Mr Toad. 'Now I have lost my spoon. I am downhearted.'

Two round tears fell from the Toad's eyes and rolled across the lily-pad into the river.

'Poor Mr Toad,' said Serena. 'We will help you to look.'

'Where did you lose it?' asked the practical Snug.

'Nowhere! It disappeared from my castle. It vanished. It faded away. One day it lay in the glass case, and the next day it had gone. Nobody came in. It went. Clean gone,' said he.

'Clean gone,' echoed Snug.

Mr Toad paddled away and the two mice filled the empty basket with flowers and went home.

'What, no fish?' cried Mr Mouse, looking at the flowers.

'Never a one,' sighed Serena. 'And Mr Toad has lost his silver spoon.'

'That magical spoon?' cried Mrs Mouse, holding up her paws in horror. 'It's a wonderful spoon.'

'Yes,' added Mr Mouse. 'If you stir your broth with it you can get any taste you like. Egg broth, chicken broth, nettle soup, dandelion soup. It doesn't matter.'

'I've heard that if you eat with that little silver spoon, you can have anything you fancy,' said Mrs Mouse. 'Cheese or bacon rinds or –'

'Wild strawberries and cream?' asked Serena.

'Anything. Anything you fancy,' said Mr Mouse.

Mrs Mouse began to sweep her clean little house. She hunted among Toad's bedclothes in the best bedroom. Mr Mouse searched the cellars. There was no sign of the silver spoon.

'How many fishes did you catch?' asked John Barleycorn.

'None,' answered Snug. 'They ate our bait.'

'Ne'er a one,' grumbled Samuel Furze. 'I wanted a sprat for my supper and you can't even catch a minnow.'

'Perhaps I shall catch a silver spoon,' said Snug hopefully.

Mrs Mouse was tired. She packed the children off to bed, and sent the three old talkative mice home.

'Good night, good night, good night,' they called, and they wandered away, peeping in the ferns and leaves for the silver spoon. The moon shone down making everything silver.

The next morning Snug and Serena set off to hunt. They turned over the pebbles and out ran creepy-crawly creatures.

'Have you seen a silver spoon?' asked Serena.

'No, sir! Please, sir! No, sir!' said the ant, Mrs Emmet. They asked the cockchafer, Jim Bassett, but he had not seen the spoon in his flight. Miss Hodmadod the snail, who sat at the door of her striped shell, said she had a silver spoon of her own so small nobody could see it.

> 'Silver spoon,
> Silver spoon.
> All things are silver,
> Under the moon,'

she sang in her wavering tiny treble.

Snug met Mr and Mrs Harvest with their caravan and baskets. They were on their way to the Fair.

'Mr Harvest,' called Snug. 'Have you got a silver spoon?'

'Can't say that I have, Snug,' said Mr Harvest. 'I've got a wooden spoon.'

'No,' added Mrs Harvest, 'but once we found one, left behind after a picnic. Oh my! It was heavy! We carried it in our caravan, and we left it at the door of the farmhouse, for a present for the new-born babby. It's lucky to have a silver spoon. They were pleased, but of course they thought it was from a fairy, and it was from us, me and him.'

'This is a silver spoon belonging to Mr Toad,' explained Serena. 'It is very little spoon, but it is magical.'

'Ah! Then it must have been took by yon fairies, as

dances by night,' said Mr Harvest.

Poor Mr Toad wandered up and down. He got quite thin and his clothes hung from his shoulders like a scarecrow's.

Mrs Dumble, his housekeeper, was worried. 'There now, Mr Toad! Don't ye take on so. It will turn up. Come and have a nice cup of tea, sir.'

'Who can have taken it?' said Mr Toad for the hundredth time.

'Who indeed? The varmint!' said Mrs Dumble.

'It isn't the Stoat or the Owl or the Weasel. It isn't the grasshopper or ladybird,' said Toad.

He peered closely at the glass case, and he saw a small mark, a scratch on the wall and a dampish patch below.

'Somebody has been here again,' said he. 'I know this mark. It's the baby Otter. There's a baby in the river for I've seen him playing with his mother. He's taken my silver spoon. I shall never get it back now. I can tackle a weasel or a stoat on occasions, but not an otter.'

'Hotters are too big. Playful a baby Hotter may be, but too big,' said Mrs Dumble, mournfully.

It was quite true. The baby Otter had stretched his sleek arm through the window and seized the bright silver spoon. He tossed it up and caught it. He licked it and he bit it. Then after a game of catch he tired of the little flashing thing. He dropped it on a lily-pad and left it, then he dived in the river to try to catch a fish.

The little fishes found the spoon on the lily. They grabbed it with their soft lips and swam with it. They strove to take it from one another. They played tug-of-war with it. At last they, too, tired of it, and down fell the silver spoon to a rock.

When Snug and Serena were told by Mr Toad that a baby Otter had taken the spoon, they knelt on the river bank and tried to see the Otter. They saw the wet round head and the bright eyes and the sleek arms of the baby Otter as it plunged and dived.

'Oh, Otter! Otter! Have you seen a silver spoon?' sang Serena in her sweetest voice.

'Is that a mermaid singing?' asked the Otter, looking round.

'It's only me, Serena. Have you seen a silver spoon?' sang Serena in her high little voice.

'Silver spoon? Yes, I left it on a lily-pad, and now it's gone,' said the Otter and he dived away.

'Let's make two new fishing-rods and fish for it,' said Snug.

So they picked some rushes and bound the handles of the rods with bindweed, and put little buns for bait from their mother's baking.

As before, the fish came whisking up and gobbled the bait in a minute.

'Oh, little fish,' called Serena. 'We don't want to catch you. We are after a silver spoon.'

'I've seen that spoon,' answered a fish. 'It's down on a rock. What will you give me if I bring it to you?'

'A pot of our mother's strawberry jam,' said Serena.

'No, our mother makes lily jam, thank you,' replied the fish.

'Cowslip wine and primrose syrup,' said Snug.

'No, we have enough wine in the river,' said the fish.

'I'll give you a little ship made out of a walnut shell, which was in my stocking at Christmas,' said Snug.

'Yes,' shouted all the fish together in silvery voices. 'Yes, a walnut-shell boat.'

So away ran Snug and Serena to their home. They fetched the walnut ship with its silk sails from Snug's bedroom. It was a treasure, but they knew they would give anything to help Mr Toad, their friend.

When they returned, the silver spoon lay on a water-lily, and all the little fishes poked their faces up to watch.

'Can't swim to it,' said Snug.

The fish then came to the bank, carrying the spoon, and Snug leaned over and took it. He floated the walnut ship on the water.

'Thank you, oh, thank you,' shrilled the little fish, and Snug and Serena danced their way home with the spoon in the fishing-basket.

There was no need to go all the way to Mr Toad's Castle. The old Toad sat in the porch of the Rose and Crown, talking to the three ancient mice. They could hear him down the garden.

'Yes, it was a magical spoon, made of pure silver, given to my ancestor by the princess.'

'A great loss,' moaned John and Samuel and Timothy.

Then down the path came Snug and Serena, carrying the basket.

'We've caught a silver fish,' they laughed to Mr Toad.

'Ah,' cried Mr Toad, rushing to them. 'What do I see? My silver spoon? Where did it come from?'

He nearly wept as he clasped the little spoon to his heart.

'From the river. The fishes gave it to us,' said Snug. He did not tell the Toad they had exchanged their treasure for it.

'Now do some magic with it,' implored Serena.

Mr Toad stroked his spoon and Snug went for a

glass of the dandelion brew. Mr Toad stirred it with his spoon, and they all had a taste. It was like cowslips and roses and oranges and strawberries all mixed in one delicious drink.

'Oh, 'larcious,' exclaimed Snug.

'Beautiful,' sighed Serena, but the three old mice finished it up at once.

'Another magic,' begged Serena.

Mr Toad dropped some dandelion seeds in the silver spoon, and blew them. They floated off like silk parachutes with butterflies flying near them.

'Now I will give a reward to the little fishes who found my spoon,' said Mr Toad.

He went to the river with Serena and Snug. He played a tune on his fiddle to summon the fish. Then he held up the spoon.

'The blessings of the wind and the sun, the moon and the earth be upon you,' said he. 'May nobody ever fish with rod or line or net in this part of the river. May you be free.'

And the strange thing was, that nobody, man or animal, could ever fish in that stretch of water again.

The Mouse Telegrams

Little fieldmice have four birthdays a year. It is a special gift from Mother Nature to make up for their small size. So Serena Mouse had a spring birthday, a summer birthday, an autumn and a winter one. Spring was a yellow birthday, summer a blue one, autumn was brown and winter snow-white.

It was Serena's spring birthday, and even Mrs Mouse had forgotten, but the cuckoo reminded her.

'Cuckoo! Cuckoo! Birthday! Birthday!' sang the bird as soon as it arrived from over the sea, and Mrs Mouse looked up from her ironing.

'Goodness me! I quite forgot little Serena!' she cried. 'Serena! Serena!' she called. 'It's your birthday, your spring birthday.'

Serena ran in from the garden, followed by Snug.

'Can we have a party?' she asked.

'Yes,' said Mrs Mouse, and she went back to her ironing.

'Oh, thank you! A birthday party, and yellow presents,' cried the little mice, dancing round their mother.

'Now do be quiet! You'll make me burn your father's shirts. I must think about this party,' said Mrs Mouse.

'Can we invite Mr Toad?' asked Serena.

'And Mr and Mrs Harvest?' added Snug.

'And little Dan Dormouse? He is my particular friend,' said Serena.

'And the gypsy hedgehogs?' asked Snug.

'Yes. They can all come if they want,' said Mrs Mouse.

'Shall we write letters to invite them?' asked Serena.

'It's too late for the post. Robin Redbreast has flown away,' said Mrs Mouse, looking rather worried.

'Shall we be postmen?' asked Snug.

'No, that is impossible,' said Mrs Mouse sadly. 'Mr Toad lives far off down by the river. The gypsy hedgehogs will be wandering with their tent and cooking-pot, visiting a fair, playing their mouth-organ. No use trying to find them.'

'And Mr and Mrs Harvest will be making baskets in their caravan. We can't find the harvest mice,' added Serena. 'Dan Dormouse will be in the woods and we shall *never* discover him.'

'Hush,' cried Mrs Mouse, putting her iron back on the fire. 'Stay quiet and let me think, for this is a puzzle.'

The little mice stayed very still listening to the thoughts of everything. The clock was ticking and that was the clock thinking. The fire was crackling and that was the fire thinking. The brook was burbling and that was the water thinking.

'Everybody's thinking,' whispered Serena.

' 'cept me,' whispered Snug.

'Well, I've had my think,' said Mrs Mouse in a soft mysterious voice. 'We will send a mouse telegram.'

'Oh! Oh!' murmured the two mice, opening wide their eyes. 'What is a mouse telegram, Mother?'

'It's an ancient quick way of sending a message,' said Mrs Mouse. 'It's a magical way, known only to animals.'

'Yes,' whispered the mice. 'Nobody but us.'

'You must pick a red-tipped daisy, and there's magic in that,' said Mrs Mouse.

'Yes,' breathed the little brown mice.

'And a double celandine, and there's a wish in that.'

'Yes,' said the mice. 'Yes, Mother.'

'And an oxlip, and there's a wish in that.'

'Yes, Mother,' said the little mice.

'And a white violet. Bring them all to me and I'll send the telegram,' said Mrs Mouse.

Off ran little Snug and Serena into the fields, peeping under leaves, peering at the petals of flowers, for magical flowers are not easy to find. In a daisyfield Serena discovered a daisy with red frilly petals. Then Snug found a double celandine growing in a wet ditch.

They ran to a cowslip field, for among cowslips there is often an oxlip, and every country child knows that a wish goes with an oxlip.

Lastly they hunted under the hedges for the first white violet.

'Here they are, Mother. Here are the telegram flowers,' called the mice as they scampered up the garden to the Rose and Crown.

Mrs Mouse tossed the blossoms up in the air for the wind to catch. As the strong South wind carried them away she called, 'Telegrams! Telegrams! Mr Toad, Mr and Mrs Harvest, Mr and Mrs Hedgehog, little Dan Dormouse. You are invited to Serena's party.'

Mr Toad got his telegram as he sat on a lily-leaf fishing in the river. 'Serena's spring birthday,' said he, and he wound up his line and shut his fishing basket. He paddled across to Toad's Castle and fetched a sack from the cellar. Then he gave a whistle and a flock of yellow butterflies flew down and entered the sack.

'Serena will like these butterflies,' said he to his housekeeper, Mrs Dumble. 'I'm off to her birthday party. Just had a telegram.'

'Take these cheesecakes,' cried Mrs Dumble, running to the larder and returning with a basket of yellow cakes.

So Mr Toad set off at his slow amble for the Rose and Crown.

Mr and Mrs Harvest were busy making baskets far away on the common when down fluttered an oxlip.

'Where has this come from?' asked Mrs Harvest, but Mr Harvest sniffed the sweet scent and knew it was a telegram.

'It's Serena's spring birthday,' said he, 'and us is asked to the party. That's a treat!'

They dabbled their paws in the stream and brushed their clothes.

'Us'll take her a rush basket with a yellow corncake inside, and a necklace of wheat ears,' said Mrs Harvest.

They packed the basket and set off for the Rose and Crown.

Mr and Mrs Hedgehog were at the village fair when a white violet fell on them from the sky.

'What does this mean, wife?' asked Mr Hedgehog.

'A white violet means good luck,' said Mrs Hedgehog.

'It means more than that,' said Mr Hedgehog. 'It's a mouse telegram, asking us to Serena's party.'

'Then we can't go,' said Mrs Hedgehog, firmly. 'We can't leave the fairground. We are too busy.'

They went back to the swings and roundabouts, calling, 'Two a penny. Take your seats,' while little animals paid their pence and swung to the music of Mr Hedgehog's mouth-organ.

Little Dan Dormouse was rolling through the leafy tunnels of a hedge when a double celandine fell on his back.

He ran home to show his mother the frill of petals.

'That's a telegram,' said Mrs Dormouse.

'What's a telegram?' asked Dan.

'A double-quick message. It is sent on double petals to get here quickly. It's an invitation to Serena's party.'

Mrs Dormouse started off to find a present. A furze bush grew like a golden fire in the hedge, and she picked some of the pea-shaped flowers. She pressed them together and she made a yellow muff just right for Serena's paws.

'Now take this present, and go carefully, with your eyes wide open for dangers,' said Mrs Dormouse as she kissed her small furry son.

Somebody else got a telegram. Snug sent a secret telegram, as he tossed a dandelion up in the air.

'Dandy-Lion, come to the party,' he sang. Then he whispered, 'I only want to know if it works.'

The wind carried off the flower, and away danced Snug.

Mr Stoat lay in his underground room, dozing with his head on a lumpy pillow. A dandelion came floating down the chimney.

'Hello,' said he, as he sniffed the strong smell. 'What's this? A telegram? An invitation to Serena's party? It's a mistake but I'll go. I'm a Dandy-Lion.'

He brushed his tawny coat and pointed his whiskers. Then he skipped up and down looking for a present.

'Ha! A mousetrap!' he muttered. 'Just right.'

At the Rose and Crown everybody was very busy,

cooking, baking, setting the table and preparing for Serena's party.

There were curdy cakes and lemon cheese tarts, orange slices and lemon buns. There was primrose wine, and cowslips in sugar, marigold buds in nectar, with buttercup ices and dried mallow cheeses. In the centre of the table was the birthday cake with lots of little candles on top, one for every happy day.

Snug walked slowly round, counting the plates. Then he put another for his dandelion guest.

He shivered as he peeped through the window. He nearly leapt out of his skin when he saw something glide round the garden like a golden lion. It stooped under the lavender bush and put a shiny present there.

'Oh dear! The S-s-s-,' stammered Snug. 'Oh dear! The Dandy-dandy-dandy! The Lion! The Lion!'

'Whatever is the matter?' asked Mrs Mouse.

'Nothing,' muttered Snug. 'It's a Dandy-dandelion out there, wanting to come in.'

'Nonsense,' said Mrs Mouse, and she looked out. 'There's nothing and nobody.'

It was true. All was quiet and the shining streak of dandelion had gone.

'There's Mr and Mrs Harvest,' called Serena, and the two harvest mice dragged their caravan to the door.

'Come in, Mr and Mrs Harvest,' said Mrs Mouse, and Mr Mouse ran up from the cellar to welcome them.

'Us wishes Serena many happy returns of the day,' said Mrs Harvest, bobbing a curtsey.

'Yes, us wishes that,' added Mr Harvest, bowing.

'Us made her a basket,' continued Mrs Harvest.

'And here her be,' added Mr Harvest, bringing the tiny rush basket from behind his back and giving it to Serena.

Mr Mouse offered the harvest mice a drink of honey wine in an acorn cup and the two sat admiring the laden table.

'Did you see a Dandy-Lion?' asked Snug.

'Lots and lots,' said Mrs Harvest, and Mr Harvest added, 'Lots and lots and lots.'

Then came a shout and a halloo, and little Dan Dormouse rolled in at the door like a furry ball. He was so entangled it took Mrs Mouse some time to set him free.

The old fieldmice came hobbling after him, waving their sticks and shouting to Mr Mouse and Serena.

'Happy birthday, everybody,' they cried.

'We've brought Serena some presents,' said Samuel Furze.

They all fumbled in their pockets and each brought out of the green depths of his trousers a tiny doll made of the white pith of rushes.

'They'll go yaller in time,' said Timothy Snout.

'How lovely,' cried Serena. 'I've never had a dolly. Thank you, dear Mr Mouses.'

The three old mice sat down at the table and began to eat.'

All this time Snug had been peering from the window, but there was no sign of the strange guest.

'Did you see a Dandy-Lion?' he asked.

'Many a one,' said the three mice, helping themselves to the food.

'There's Mr Toad,' cried Serena, running down the path to meet the stout animal.

'Happy birthday, my dear,' said Mr Toad, and he untied the sack. Out flew the cloud of brimstone butterflies, dancing in a circle round Serena's head.

She clapped her paws in delight, and when Mr Toad went indoors she stayed in the garden, watching the pretty flock. They fluttered across the grass and entered a little wire house which lay under the lavender bush. They sipped the piece of honeycomb which lay inside.

'What is this?' cried Serena. 'A house for me!'

She ran inside singing:

> 'Just the house for me!
> Just the house for me!
> A little wee house,
> Just right for a mouse,
> And honeycomb for tea!'

There was a snap! The door shut, and she was caught in the mousetrap.

Out from the bushes came the Stoat, and away flew the butterflies in a fright. The Stoat picked up the little mousetrap, with Serena inside and rushed off with it under his arm.

'Mother! Mother! Mr Toad! Oh! Oh!' cried Serena.

'Don't be frightened,' said the Stoat. 'You are safe with me.'

'I want to go home to my party,' sobbed Serena, running up and down and beating her small fists against the wires. 'Let me go, naughty Stoat.'

The Stoat dashed on. He ran down the passage and put the mousetrap on the floor of his house.

'Now Serena, here you will live, and you may as well stop crying for you can't escape,' said he. 'I always wanted a nice little fieldmouse to sing to me. Sing that song about the house.'

'I can't,' sobbed Serena. 'Let me go or Mr Toad will come after you and my father will bring a big stick and beat you, and Snug will bite you.'

'Why, it was Snug who invited me to your party,' said the Stoat. 'He sent a mouse telegram of a Dandy-Lion to me.'

Serena was so startled she said. no more. She crouched in a corner of the trap and wept little tears that rolled out like pearls.

'I can't abide a weeping mouse,' said the Stoat, crossly. 'I'm going out, and mind your tears are dried when I come back. I don't like a wet floor!'

He leapt over the heap of bones, shut the door and locked it after him, and away he went.

Serena tried to raise the catch of the mousetrap, but she was too feeble. She called, but the Stoat's house was underground, and nobody could hear her little squeaks.

There was a flutter in the chimney and down to the ugly room came the flock of golden butterflies, like sunshine and primroses floating there.

'Oh, save me! Save me!' cried Serena, and the butterflies darted around her and then flew back up the chimney. Soon they returned with a long green thread of plaited grasses, which they tied in a butterfly bow to the side of the mousetrap.

The butterflies pulled in a dancing, wavering crowd, but the trap did not move.

'Of course you can't help me,' sighed Serena. 'You are not strong enough.'

Up the chimney they flew again with the end of the thread, out into the wood. Mr Toad waited there, near the chimney, among the grasses he had plaited so neatly. He wrapped the end of the thread round his own stout body and then he pulled, slowly walking away. The mousetrap jerked and bumped across the bony floor of the Stoat's house, and up the chimney with little Serena rattling like a pea inside it. Up to the woodland it came, and Mr Toad unfastened the door. Little Serena escaped from her prison.

'Oh, Mr Toad! You have saved me, you and all the yellow butterflies!' she cried, embracing the fat old Toad, while the brimstones danced in the air around her head.

'Quick! Quick! No time to lose,' murmured Mr Toad, and he took her trembling hand and hurried her away.

'How did you know where I was?' she panted.

'I followed the butterflies,' said Mr Toad.

'I came as fast as I could toddle, for I knew where Mr Stoat lives. I couldn't get down the chimney, of course, so I sent a rope by the butterflies when Mr Stoat left the house.'

'Serena! Where have you been?' asked Mrs Mouse.

'She was took,' said the Toad, pointing a finger at Snug. 'She was took by a Dandy-Lion!'

Snug hung his head. 'I'm sorry, Serena. I never knew. I never thought.'

Serena was so glad to get home she could not speak. She sat down at the table and drank ten cups of tea and ate a candle, she was so hungry. The old mice had finished off everything except the candles on the cake.

'Where did you go?' whispered Snug.

'I'll tell you later,' murmured Serena, taking up another yellow candle and nibbling it.

So when all the guests had gone home, and the tea things were washed up, Serena told her story. Mr Toad stayed behind to hear and he nodded his head as she talked.

'Mouse telegrams are dangerous things,' said he. 'You never know if the right people will get them.'

Snug and Serena Count Twelve

'Snug and Serena ought to go to school,' said Mrs Mouse one day. The two little mice put down their spoons and listened. Their eyes shone, their tails twitched, and they licked their lips with excitement.

'School? What for?' asked Mr Mouse.

'To learn things,' said Mrs Mouse.

'What things?' demanded Mr Mouse. 'They can learn enough at home without going to school. They can fetch and carry, and run errands. They can sweep the floor, and dust the chairs, and make rush mats as well as anybody. They can carve chestnuts into baskets, and polish hazel nuts and collect cherry stones.'

Snug and Serena opened wide their eyes as Mr Mouse told of their cleverness. He had never mentioned it before.

'That is not enough,' said Mrs Mouse, firmly.

'What else?' asked Mr Mouse, impatiently. 'They can find herbs and bring them home to make dandelion wine and herb tea, and nettle beer, and wild thyme ointment.'

'Go on with your breakfasts,' said Mrs Mouse to Snug and Serena, and they went on.

'They ought to know how to count,' said Mrs Mouse.

'I can teach 'em to count,' said Mr Mouse, gruffly. He went to the dresser and took down the blue mugs.

'One mug for John Barleycorn,' said he, thumping a mug on the table.

'One for Jonathan Furze, and one for Samuel.'

He went on banging the table with a mug as he spoke.

'That's three mugs.'

'That's only counting up to three,' objected Mrs Mouse. 'There's more than three in the world.'

Mr Mouse ran to the dresser where the blue mugs were ranged in a row.

'One mug for Mr Toad, and one for you, my dear. That's five mugs,' said he, triumphantly, as he banged down two more mugs.

Snug and Serena giggled, but Mr Mouse frowned at them.

'There's more mugs left, William,' said Mrs Mouse, quietly. 'Go on with your counting.'

Mr Mouse stamped across the floor and took two more mugs.

'A mug for Snug and one for Serena to drink new milk in,' said he. 'That's two mugs.'

'No, it's seven,' said Snug. 'Mr Toad told me.'

'No mouse has ever been known to count more than five,' said Mr Mouse. 'After five we begin again. We've had five, and now we begin again. A Toad may count more but Mouses don't.'

'Let us go to school, please,' cried Serena. 'We want to count lots and lots.'

'We will ask Mr Toad for advice,' said Mrs Mouse. 'He will know about such things.'

All that day Snug and Serena scampered about counting things. When they got up to five they hesitated and when they got to seven they stopped.

'Mr Toad will help us,' they said.

Next day Mr Toad came and Serena ran to meet him.

'Well, little Serena, you are in a hurry,' said Mr Toad, pleasantly, and he put his thumbs in his waistcoat and looked at the eager little Mouse. Snug came hurrying after her.

'Please, Mr Toad, I want to go to school,' said Serena, 'and so does Snug. Both of us. One, two of us.'

'I'll give you some lessons,' said Mr Toad, puffing out his chest.

'We want to do counting,' said Serena.

'Counting? Why?' asked the fat old Toad. 'I've already taught you to count up to seven, which is the magic number. Seven stars in the Great Bear up in the sky. Seven nuts in a hazel bunch. Seven cows in our field. Seven pigs in the pigsty. Seven mugs on your dresser.'

'We want to know how many rooks are flying and how many bees in a swarm,' said Serena.

'And how many blackbirds in the hedges, and how many worms in the ground,' added Snug.

'And how many fish in the river,' said Serena, 'and how many frogs in the marsh, and how many toads . . . toads . . . toads . . .'

'There is only one toad and that's me,' said Mr Toad. 'The others don't count. And there's only one Policeman Owl in the wood but there's a Hunting Owl in the lane. He doesn't count.

Luckily only one fierce Stoat lives in that house in the rocks.'

He hesitated and looked down at the two small mice.

'I know a clever animal who will teach you to count,' said he, kindly. 'It is true I only count up to seven but this animal knows more. She's a bit strange in her ways, a foreigner, but she can count. I am not sure, indeed I am not sure, but perhaps . . . perhaps . . .'

He went with the two little mice into the Rose and Crown.

Mr Mouse was polishing the blue mugs and saying, 'One, two, three, four, five. One, two. That makes sense, that does. Where does seven come in?'

Mrs Mouse was calming him down.

'Oh, Mr Toad,' she cried, as Mr Toad, with Snug and Serena hanging on to his coat tails, entered.

'Yes, I know,' said Mr Toad. 'It's the schooling, isn't it?'

'Yes, will you give us some advice?' asked Mr Mouse. 'Snug says you have taught him to count seven. He says there are seven mugs on my dresser.'

'Mr Mouse, William,' began Mr Toad. 'I think you ought to let your children go to school and learn to count. I know of a teacher, a clever animal, but . . . but . . . she's different from us.'

'In what way?' asked Mrs Mouse, anxiously.

'She's a refugee. She's away from home. She's a town mouse living in the country,' said Mr Toad.

'Poor thing,' said Mrs Mouse. 'A refugee.'

'She pines for her own life, but she dare not return. She came to live here a week ago. She is very clever. She could teach our little Mouses to count,' said Mr Toad.

He talked it over privately with Mr and Mrs Mouse, and they agreed to send Snug and Serena to the Town Mouse's cottage.

'She is very sharp and quick-tempered, but she has a lot of knowledge through living in the same house as Human Beings,' said Mr Toad.

'In the same house as those giants?' cried Mr Mouse.

'Yes, it's her house, but she allows them to live there. However, Somebody Else came there and she found she couldn't share her house with the – er – er – Somebody Else,' said Mr Toad. 'So she packed her bag and came to the lane, to take an empty cottage under the foxgloves.'

Mr and Mrs Mouse nodded.

'You can trust her. She has a birch rod for discipline, and a corner for naughty mice, and she can count,' said Mr Toad.

'Well, I agree to that,' said Mr Mouse. 'Some discipline will do Snug and Serena good. As for counting, well, let them count.'

So Snug and Serena prepared for school. They went to the woods to find pencils and slates. The pencils were sharp pointed little sticks with which they could write in the sandy ground. The slates were thin layers of shale from a cutting in the old quarry. Snug and Serena found half a dozen little square slabs of stone, thin as wafers, all ready for use. There were many more stored under the grassy edge of the sandstone.

'We can write on these with some bits of hard stone,' said Snug, and they picked up some splinters of stone and scribbled on the slates.

Mrs Mouse knew where there was a pile of cherry stones bleached by the sun, smooth as ivory. They had been left by the field mice when they ate the fallen wild cherries in the woods.

'These are for counting,' said she, and Snug and Serena filled two school bags with them.

There was a bat's-wing purse to hold their school money, and a bag of netting to hold their slates and pencils. The school money was mice money, which is the seeds of buttercups and chervil and other plants.

Snug and Serena were washed and scrubbed. Snug had a new handkerchief and Serena a new pinafore, so they looked neat and pretty as they set off to school with Mrs Mouse and Mr Toad to take them there on the first day.

They all went down the lane, through a foxglove archway to a small cottage hidden in the bank among ferns and mosses.

Mrs Town Mouse, who felt the draughts of the country, had brought in sheep's wool to make carpets and curtains, and pieces of wood for floors, and pieces of waste paper for bedding.

Mr Toad rapped at the door and Mrs Mouse sniffed a little.

'Stuffy,' said she. 'Not enough fresh air for a country mouse.'

Mrs Town Mouse answered the door. She was delighted to see company, and she invited them all inside.

'I have brought my children to be your pupils,' said Mrs Mouse, softly. 'Mr Toad said you would teach them to count.'

'Certainly,' said Mrs Town Mouse, looking at Snug and Serena with her sharp little eyes. 'I am a great counter. I shall be glad to teach your pretty children.'

'Then I will leave them in your charge, thank you. Send them home in good time for dinner, Mrs Town Mouse. They have their school money in their purses,' said Mrs Mouse.

Mrs Mouse and Mr Toad went away and Snug and Serena were left. Snug darted round the room looking at everything and Serena began to dance.

'Stop!' cried Mrs Town Mouse. 'Sit still! I can't teach you if you dance about like this. You must learn to be quiet.'

She was so stern the two mice sat silently on the low seats.

They had to keep so still they thought they would be changed into stone.

'When a fierce animal looks at you, he won't see you if you keep still,' said Mrs Town Mouse, severely. 'You must first learn to be still.'

'A hawk once carried me off,' said Snug, jumping up. 'I got home again, and I left my jacket behind on the church steeple.'

'Silence!' cried Mrs Town Mouse. 'It is possible to escape from a hawk, but you could not get away from a cat.'

'Please, can we do counting?' piped Serena. 'I don't want to hear about cats.'

Mrs Town Mouse frowned. 'A cat is a very fierce animal. It eats the mice in one gulp. It is an ogre, a dragon, and its eyes are like green fires. Its teeth are like white swords, and its tongue like a red flame.'

'I should like to meet a cat,' said Snug. 'I'm not afraid. Now let's go on to counting.'

'You boastful mouse,' said Mrs Town Mouse, crossly.

She trotted away and fetched her bead frame for counting. Serena and Snug emptied their cherry stones from their bags. The lesson began.

The mice made little piles of white cherry stones, and Mrs Town Mouse counted with them. She taught them a song as they darted here and there carrying the little stones.

'One, two, three, four,
Mouses at their mother's door.
Five, six, seven, eight,
Cherry stones are on a plate.
Nine, ten, eleven, twelve,
Mouses dig and mouses delve.
Twelve's a dozen, please remember,
All the months till cold December.'

'That's enough for today,' said Mrs Town Mouse. 'You have learned a dozen, and that is a big number.'

'How many stars in the sky?' asked Snug, collecting his cherry stones and putting them back in his bag.

'Lots of dozens. Lots of twelves,' said Mrs Town Mouse.

'How many fishes in the river?' asked Serena.

'You must go there and find out,' said Mrs Town Mouse, impatiently.

'The three old Mice went fishing with my father and caught some big ones,' said Snug.

'Don't talk about fish,' shuddered the Town Mouse. 'We had plenty of fish in our house, but it was food for the Cat. Don't mention it.'

'Can we talk about stars?' asked Serena. 'Did your Cat eat stars?'

'She might,' said the Town Mouse. 'She prowled at night when the stars came out and sometimes she and her friends gave a concert of horrible music on the roof. She sang so loudly we shivered in our home under the floor.'

'Come again tomorrow,' said the Town Mouse, as they paid their mouse pennies. 'I will teach you to count more numbers.'

'I like counting,' said Snug. 'I'm glad there are more numbers to learn.'

'Goodbye, Mrs Town Mouse,' said Serena. 'Have we been good?'

'Yes, fairly good,' said the Town Mouse, and she yawned. The two little mice tripped away.

They sang their counting song, but somehow they got it all wrong.

> 'One, two, three, four,
> Pussy at the mouse's door.
> Five, six, seven, eight,
> Eating mouses off a plate.
> Nine, ten, eleven, twelve,
> Pussy smiles and licks herself.
> Mouses gone and so are we,
> We are going home to tea.'

They went along the lane, chattering about numbers and they counted the things they saw. One robin sang its gay song, and two cuckoos shouted, 'Cuckoo,' in the wood.'

Three crows flew across the sky, and four snails crept among the leaves.

Five calves looked over a wall, and six pigeons sat in a high fir tree.

Seven little rabbits danced on the common, and eight baby moorhens swam in the stream.

Nine frogs hopped in the marsh, and ten butterflies flitted overhead.

Eleven ants searched on the ground and twelve bees were making honey.

They dawdled among the company of birds and insects, the flowers and small animals, counting and singing a new song, much easier than Mrs Town Mouse's.

'One robin in a tree,
Two cuckoos shout to me.
Three crows up in the sky,
Four snails come crawling by.
Five calves look o'er a wall,
Six pigeons croon and call.
Seven rabbits on the green,
Eight moorhens swim the stream.
Nine frogs in marshy bed,
Ten butterflies overhead.
Eleven ants look for money,
Twelve bees are after honey.'

They got home at last. It was late and Mrs Mouse
was at the door looking for them.

'Here you come. Mrs Town Mouse kept you a long time,' said Mrs Mouse. 'Have you had any dinner?'

'Oh, yes. We had twelve wild strawberries, and eleven pots of honey, and ten sips of water and nine drops of honeydew, and eight blades of grass and seven loaves of bee-bread,' began Snug in a hurry.

'We can count, Mother, up to twelve,' said Serena, excitedly. 'We've been counting all the way home. Everything is part of counting.'

'Well, come in and have your tea, and count the slices of bread and butter,' laughed Mrs Mouse. 'Mr Toad has been waiting to see you.'

The old Toad rose to his feet as they entered.

'My little Serena! My little Snug!' said he. 'I have been worried about you. Was the Town Mouse easy with you? Did she use the birch rod?'

'Oh, no, Mr Toad. She was kind and she taught us lots of counting,' said Serena.

'One Mr Toad. Two little brown mice. Three old mice,' began Snug as Samuel and Timothy and John Barleycorn came in to hear the news.

'Four cups on the table, five chairs in the kitchen, six candles in the cupboard, seven mugs on the dresser,' said Serena, hurriedly.

'Stop! Don't count any more. I feel dizzy,' said Mr Mouse, as he brought a bottle of sweet primrose wine from the cellar for the three old mice to sip.

They all sat round the table, eight of them, and Mrs Mouse gave them wild strawberry jam and little cheese cakes, and rolls of wheat bread with sorrel leaves for salad.

Afterwards Snug and Serena sang the song the Town Mouse had taught them, but it was still all wrong.

'One, two, three, four,
Weasels tapping at my door.
Five, six, seven, eight,
Stoats and owls are never late.
Nine, ten, eleven, twelve,
Mouses dig and Mouses delve.'

'We know that song,' said the Old Mice. 'Listen to us.' They croaked and wheezed, and sang in shrill high trebles:

'One, two, three four,
Harvest mice upon the floor.
Five, six, seven, eight,
Eating bread and cheese and
                    mate.
Nine, ten, eleven, twelve,
If you want any more you must
    sing it yourselves.'

'How many stars in the sky, Snug?' asked Mr Toad, slyly, when the two little mice were ready for bed.

'Dozens and dozens,' said Snug.

'Mrs Town Mouse is going to count them for us,' said Serena.

'Then you'll want lots of cherry stones,' said Mr Toad.

But Mrs Town Mouse did not count them, nor did Snug and Serena have any more lessons from her.

'Too-whit. Too-whoo,' cried the Owl that night, and he flew down the lane with his white wings spread, as he hunted for a nice fat mouse.

Mrs Town Mouse shivered and pulled the curtains close and locked the door.

'Too-whit. Too-whoo,' hooted the Owl. 'I've heard there's a fat town mouse down here.'

Mrs Mouse began to pack her clothes and her bits of things.

'Sniff! Sniff!' went the Stoat. 'There's a town mouse all stout and plump. I must catch her tomorrow.'

The Stoat ruffled the leaves in the hedge bottom, and Mrs Mouse crouched in the depths of her hole.

At dawn she ventured out. She carried her belongings in a bag and ran as fast as she could back to the town house.

'A Cat in the kitchen is better than an Owl in the lane and a Stoat at your door,' said she, as she slipped through a hole in the all. 'There's better food at home. I'm going back.'

So that is why Snug and Serena never counted the stars in the sky or the fish in the river or the daisies in the fields.

'You know quite enough for two little field mice,' said Mr Toad. 'I'll teach you the names of the stars.'

He began at the Great Bear and he told them about the Dog Star, and the Swan, the Heavenly Twins and Pegasus the Horse. The little mice with their bright eyes could see these great pictures in the starry sky and they did not trouble to count the stars.

Snug and Serena Go to Town

'Serena,' cried Snug one day, as the two little fieldmice sat in a meadow, sunning their bright fur, and looking at the blue sky. 'Serena, I've been thinking.'

'And what have you thought?' asked Serena, turning round from her perch on a dandelion flower and looking at her brother. He sat with his head upturned in his paws. Yes, he was thinking hard, Serena could tell that.

'I've been thinking I would like to go and see Mrs Town Mouse,' said Snug, and his words astonished Serena so much she rolled off the dandelion and nearly fell on top of her brother.

She picked a petal of the dandelion and put it across her lips and blew a sound like that of a tiny trumpet.

'Why?' she asked. 'Why, oh why?' she squeaked.

'To find where she lives, and to see the big humans and the cat and all the things she spoke about, and to learn another number. What comes after twelve, Serena?'

'I don't know, but let's go and find out,' said Serena.

'Don't tell anyone,' she added, 'not even Mr Toad, or they will stop us. You know what grown-up mice are like, always afraid of something. Be careful! Cats! Weasels!'

They went home and packed their bags. Mrs Mouse was out and Mr Mouse was down in the cellar making dandelion wine. They only took a clean handkerchief, a toothbrush and pyjamas. Then off they went the same morning.

They didn't walk. Oh no! A laundry van was waiting down the lane with a nice brown horse. They climbed in at the back and got into the laundry basket. Then the man returned and the horse trotted off and Snug and Serena were shaken down to the bottom of the basket, all among the towels and sheets. It was warm and sweet-smelling and very comfortable. The linen basket was not going to Mrs Mouse's house, that would have been too wonderful for real life, but they had a good ride to the town, and when the van delivered the clean clothes to a house, Snug and Serena climbed out.

They were in a big, untidy kitchen, with plenty of food sprinkled on the floor and on the table, which was just what they liked. So they feasted. The door was opened and a lady came in. They hid under a frilly chair. Unluckily two cats also entered the kitchen and for a moment there was a panic as the little mice watched them. Snug and Serena shrank into the shadows, but one cat went under the chair and the little mice were obliged to squeeze themselves into a crack in the wall.

'Martha, I think I smell mousies,' said the cat to her friend.

'Yes, Tibbie,' said the other cat, 'but I'm not hungry. Don't let's bother. Come and talk to me. How is that traveller of yours, Mrs Town Mouse, going on?' Tibbie lay down and began to wash her paws.

'Oh, very well,' said she. 'Since she came back from the country she sits by the kitchen fire counting, and how she boasts! She tells tales of country mice and how she taught two of them. I don't believe a word.'

'Nor do I,' said Martha.

'She said she had a school in her cottage in the country and she taught these mice. They were clever little things, but skinny, and their names were Snug and Serena.'

'What a tale to tell!' said Martha.

'She said they were so clever and sweet they easily counted up to twelve. She said she received mouse money and a certain Mr Toad paid her respectful compliments.'

'I don't believe a word of it,' said Martha. 'Why did she come back here?'

'Because,' said the cat, 'the country was cold and it rained and she missed the excitement of dodging cats.'

'Ah,' pondered Martha, and then she started, for she heard a little voice coming from the wainscot.

'Please, Mrs Cat, please,' squeaked Snug.

'Please, Mrs Cat, where does she live?' squeaked Serena.

'Sh-sh-sh. Mice squealing,' cried the cats and they sprang like tigers at the hole in the wall.

'Where does she live,' asked faint, high voices as the mice backed deeper in their hole.

'She lives next door, young mice, but if you like to come out I'll show you the way.' The cats smiled and licked their lips.

'No, thank you,' said Snug softly.

'Later on,' added Serena.

All was safe in the hole and they combed their whiskers and curled their tails and settled down to sleep, lulled by the purring cats.

In the morning, as soon as the housewife came down and opened the door, the cats ran out and after them trotted the little mice. They went down the path, round the fence and into the garden next door. The door was shut but they saw a drain pipe, so they ran into it and climbed up it. A shower of water washed them down but they rubbed their eyes and tried again, and finally when all was quiet they found themselves in the kitchen of the Next Door.

This was a little kitchen with no food on the floor and no crumbs on the table; Snug found a cake of scented soap which he nibbled and Serena found some biscuits in an open tin.

They were both enjoying themselves when they heard a rustle, and there on the floor sat Mrs Town Mouse holding up her paws in surprise.

'Well, I never! Isn't it Snug and Serena?' she asked.

'Yes, Ma'am,' cried Snug, and Serena ran and kissed her.

'Welcome, my children! Have you come to see your old teacher?' asked the Town Mouse.

'Yes, we wanted to see you again,' said Snug, and Serena nodded and hugged the Town Mouse even tighter.

'It isn't safe here,' said the Town Mouse, nervously. 'Tibbie, the cat, sometimes brings her friend Martha to the kitchen. Come to my own apartments.'

She led the way through a small hole in the floor and the two mice followed her. They went along passages, full of dust and dirt, with now and then a spider or a black beetle sitting in the shadows. Mrs Mouse hurried along until she came to a door. She pushed the cobweb curtain and they saw a nice little room, all cosily furnished with a bed and a table and chest of drawers and a hook for clothes.

Mrs Mouse made up two little beds in the passage and invited the mice to stay as long as they liked.

'I get lonely all day by myself,' said she. 'I shall be glad to have your company. I've married since I saw you, but Mr Town Mouse is a very busy mouse, out all day.'

So there they stayed and Mrs Mouse taught them the rules of a town house. They must stay indoors till it was night, they must watch out for the cats and human beings, they must never touch a trap.

'But where can we drink the dew and nibble flowers and play with the other fieldmice?' asked Serena.

'Not here,' said the Town Mouse. 'We have other joys. You shall dance on velvet carpets and frisk on cushions and lick a silver spoon and sleep in a fur coat – and you shall see something special, and hear music, too.'

'Oh,' said Serena, 'oh – oh!' and she began to sing:

> 'Silk and fur and satin,
> Cotton, velvet, rags.
> She has married a rich mouse
> With money in his bags.'

'Silence!' cried Mrs Town Mouse. 'The cat will hear you.'

Mrs Mouse gave them a good meal of meat and pudding which she took from her larder shelf. They sipped cream and ate little sugar biscuits and chocolates, all stored by the careful Town Mouse in her larder.

Dusk was falling when Mrs Town Mouse took them to a concert. She carried a basket of scraps of paper and coloured cotton on her arm. She led the two mice through many passages to a round hole of a doorway which went to the sitting-room. A bright light shone and Mrs Mouse whispered, 'Hush! Hush!' Somebody was singing and playing the piano. Snug and Serena listened enchanted. Sometimes they couldn't resist joining in with thin, high squeaks. 'Tra-la-la,' they sang. 'Tra-la-la, tirra-lirra-lee.'

tra-la-la...

The piano stopped and a voice said, 'What was that? I thought I heard a ghostly tra-la-la, tirra-lirra.'

'Only an echo, my dear,' answered a gruff voice. 'Do go on with your delightful song.'

'Where does the music come from?' asked Serena, and she pushed her little head through the hole and took a good look at the piano, the lady and the bright lights. She had never seen anything like it in the fields and the woods of home, or even in the kitchen of the Rose and Crown when the three old mice were singing to the music of a straw pipe and a tiny drum.

Suddenly she darted into the room and Snug followed after, to the horror of the Town Mouse. Snug and Serena ran under the piano and stayed there listening. Then when the music stopped they climbed the piano legs and ran across the shiny surface and disappeared among the wires inside. There they sat, but no more music was played, so reluctantly they crept out again and went back to Mrs Town Mouse who was in a terrible fright.

'You naughty mice!' she scolded. 'You must never do that again! Wait here till the lights go out and then you can explore.' There was more music and the little mice listened with joy; then the company went out of the room and the three mice crept through the door in the wainscot, they climbed up the piano legs and entered the piano.

Snug and Serena plucked the strings and a delicious little twang came from them. They nibbled the red felts of the keys and then they ran to the keyboard and slid along the smooth, white ivories. The dance on the piano keys was the best of all and they made a tinkling duet, Serena in the treble, and Snug in the bass.

Mrs Mouse seemed very busy. She carried her basket of scraps into the piano and wove them into a heap which already lay there. She worked so hard nibbling the felts of the piano and running to her pile that the little mice went to watch her.

'What are you making, Mrs Town Mouse?' asked Serena.

'A nest, my child,' said Mrs Mouse mysteriously. 'A nest for – '

'For robins?' asked Serena.

'For tom-tits?' asked Snug.

'No, for mousies,' said Mrs Town Mouse. 'But it is time to return home. My dear husband will be waiting for me and you have not met him yet.'

They all scampered down through the doorway into the long passage to the Town Mouse's house.

Mr Mouse had just arrived. He smiled at the two eager little mice and said he was glad to see them for he had heard fine stories of their counting.

Then he opened a bag which he had put on the floor.

'I had a good haul today, my dear Evangeline,' said he to Mrs Town Mouse. 'I found a rag-bag hanging in a shed so I helped myself to some pretty scraps of scarlet and blue for the nest.'

He showed his bits and pieces and then, while Mrs Mouse prepared supper, he went to the passage and along the path to the piano.

It was a grand night, for after supper he sang to the little mice and played a straw flute and he tapped with his feet on a drum made out of a cotton reel. They all went early to bed, but they arose at day-break and went to the kitchen to collect food.

The cat was out so Snug and Serena, with Mr and Mrs Town Mouse, collected a basket full of cheese from the shelf and bread from the bread bin, of cake from the larder and bacon rinds and soap.

Later, when Mr Town Mouse had gone out to work, Mrs Mouse gave Snug and Serena a lesson. She told them that there was a new number which came after twelve. It was thirteen, a very important number, which might be lucky and might be unlucky. Mrs Town Mouse made twelve little balls of bread and then she told Snug to make another little ball. 'That's thirteen,' she said.

Then Mrs Mouse took twelve currants from a blue paper bag and placed them on the table; Serena fetched another. 'That's thirteen,' said Snug.

Just then the cat strolled in and they scuttled through the hole.

'I told you thirteen could be unlucky,' said Mrs Mouse. 'We only just escaped in time. Beware of thirteen, my dears.'

Serena put her head through the hole and watched the cat Tibbie who walked upon the table staring at the thirteen little heaps.

'What is she up to now?' murmured Tibbie.

Mrs Mouse took them for a short walk in the street but Snug and Serena did not like the boots walking past.

She showed them the rose tree by the drain-pipe and told them that if they climbed up it they could get into a bedroom and sleep on a real feather pillow. Then she took them home to dinner.

In the afternoon she gave them a book to read or to eat. They could do exactly as they pleased. She said she was going back to the nest to add some feathers which she had found.

She was gone a long time. Snug and Serena read the book and then they ate the corners; they nibbled at a piece of chocolate and then they ventured through the hole to the kitchen. The clock stood in the corner and Serena climbed to the top. Then the clock whirred and struck one, two, three with a loud noise. Down fell little Serena in a fright.

'The clock struck three
And down fell she,
Dickory-dickory-dock,'

sang Serena. But the cats walked in and it wasn't safe so she ran back to the hole where Snug was waiting for her.

'I wish she would come,' said Serena. 'I feel lonely. I should like to see Mr Toad.'

At last there was soft swish of skirts and Mrs Mouse came round the corner. She had a strange expression on her face. She was smiling as if she had a secret.

'Here I am, children. Now come with me. It is time you had your music lesson. What was the number I taught you?'

'Thirteen,' said Serena.

'Remember thirteen, my dears,' said she.

She led them down the passages to the music room and across the soft carpet into the piano, but instead of letting them play on the ivory keys she took them to the nest.

What did they see? A crowd of little pink babies lay there, all curled up and sleeping happily.

'There! My babies! Count them! Aren't they beautiful?' cried Mrs Town Mouse, proudly.

'Not very beautiful,' murmured Serena under her breath and Snug grunted crossly, but they counted the little creatures.

'Thirteen, Mrs Mouse,' said Snug and Serena.

'Quite right, my dears,' said Mrs Mouse. 'I shall

have to make thirteen little beds with pillows.'

'Where will they sleep?' asked Serena, uneasily.

'Oh, we can easily put thirteen beds in the room,' said Mrs Mouse. 'They will only stay in the piano till their eyes are opened. It is too noisy here for them. I wonder what Mr Mouse will say.'

Mr Mouse was rather astonished at the number but he was glad to see his family. 'Thirteen and Snug makes fourteen and Serena makes fifteen children,' said he.

From that moment Snug and Serena had to work like slaves. They found feathers to make the cots and they nibbled paper to make the sheets. They went to the kitchen with baskets for food. They washed the babies and dressed them in little nightgowns.

'I didn't come here to be a nursemaid,' grumbled Snug, as he made the cots and tidied the passage, and swept away the spiders.

'I wish we had some counting to do,' said Serena, as she rocked the babies and soothed their cries and wails.

'Have you counted them lately, Serena?' asked Snug. 'There's thirteen, you know.'

'Yes, a big number,' agreed Serena. 'I count them every day and they are always thirteen.' said Snug. 'I don't think I like that.'

Then one day when Serena counted there were only twelve. Could it be possible? Had she made a mistake? She went through them again but there were still only twelve. Although she swept under the beds and hunted in the corners, little Thirteen had vanished.

'Where's Thirteen?' asked Mrs Mouse, very crossly.

'Gone,' said Snug.

'Vanished,' said Serena.

Then Mrs Mouse spied a little bonnet lying in the hole and when she peeped through Martha was licking her lips.

'Any more, Mrs Town Mouse?' she asked. 'That was a delicious morsel.'

Poor Mrs Town Mouse nearly fainted.

'Well, you've twelve left,' said Mr Town Mouse cheerfully. 'I always thought thirteen was an unlucky number.'

'Oh, my Thirteen, the prettiest baby of the family,' sighed Mrs Town mouse.

'Twelve left,' said Serena, calmly.

'That's subtraction,' said Mrs Mouse, wiping her eyes. 'One from thirteen leaves twelve.'

Snug and Serena whispered together, 'Subtraction means taking away.'

'I don't want to be subtracted by a cat,' added Serena, shivering.

That night, when all the twelve were asleep and Mr and Mrs Town Mouse were snoring, Snug and Serena decided to go home.

'We shall be subtracted if we stay here much longer,' said Snug.

They found their ragged toothbrushes which Mrs Mouse had used to clean the grate. They looked for their handkerchiefs but they had disappeared as dusters. Their pyjamas had been torn to shreds for the babies' cots.

Then, waving a paw to Mr and Mrs Mouse who were fast asleep, they set off. They climbed into a laundry basket and lay till morning. They could hear the two cats snuffing around but they kept very still. The basket was lifted high on the laundry-man's shoulder and carried away. It was dumped in the van and the horse trotted off. So they went through the town back to the country.

When they reached the corner by the fields the van stopped. The laundry-man put the basket on the ground while he locked the van door. Like a flash

Snug and Serena squeezed out and hid in the grass. They knew where they were; the familiar smells of the country lane came to them, the scent of May blossom, bluebells and violets, of moss and wet leaves. They ran towards home and on their way they saw Mr Toad who walked with his head bent and his shoulders sagging.

'Oh, Mr Toad!' cried Serena.

'Oh, dear Mr Toad!' called Snug.

'Oh, my little Serena and Snug!' cried the old Toad, and he sobbed and wiped his eyes and put his hand on his heart. 'How good it is to see you again! I thought you had gone for ever. Come along home to your mother and father. They have been so unhappy, my dears. Mrs Mouse cried so much she made a stream by the door and I had to build a bridge over it so that the three old mice could come and cry with us.'

What a welcome there was to the truants! They sat round the fire with their parents and the old mice, telling their strange story, and Mrs Mouse filled up their basins of bread and milk as she listened.

'So now you can count thirteen,' said Mr Toad.

'Yes, and we can do subtraction,' laughed Snug. 'We subtracted ourselves from Mrs Town Mouse's family.'

Alison Uttley
Tales of Little Grey Rabbit £1.50

At last – the classic you've been waiting for! A loud cheer for Little Grey
Rabbit and her friends Hare, Squirrel, Moldy Warp and Fuzzypeg the
hedgehog. Together for the first time, four stories which tell of their exciting
adventures and escapades. Introducing the enemies, Fox and Weasel and a
host of endearing animal characters. A book to be treasured.

Antoine de Saint-Exupéry
The Little Prince £1.25

The Little Prince comes to earth to learn the secret of what is really important
in life. He tells an air pilot in the Sahara Desert what he has learned, in stories
about the planet where he lives – stories about a haughty flower, his fight
with the bad seeds, and other planets and their rulers.

Patricia Cleveland-Peck
The String Family 95p

The miniature world of the String family – Mr and Mrs String, their children, Hemp, Flax, Twine and baby Skein all come alive and share their adventures with Sally in Miss Floribunda's cottage in the country. Sally is the only human child to be introduced to the String family and friends – a wonderland of aunts and cousins with exciting and exotic names – the Binder-Twines, the Garden-Lines and the Embroidery-Silks.

The String Family in Summer £1.00

The String family live very happily amongst the old-fashioned dinner service on top of the dresser which belongs to Miss Floribunda, the owner of Willow Cottage. Mr and Mrs String have their work cut out preventing their lively children – Hemp, Flax, Twine and baby Skein – from being tied up in knots! They also have to cope with a variety of aunts and cousins who all have exotic-sounding names – the Binder-Twines, the Garden-Lines, and the Embroidery-Silks!

Ann Lawrence
Oggy and the Holiday 90p

Both Oggy the hedgehog and Tiggy the kitten enjoy the new experience of a seaside holiday where they meet some new and interesting friends.

All good things must come to an end – the friends say goodbye – but somehow Oggy gets left behind . . .

The Travels of Oggy 95p

Oggy is a young unadventurous hedgehog who lives very happily in a garden near Hampstead Heath which belongs to 'his' family. But when his family move to the country, Oggy gets lonely and decides to follow them . . .

Sinéad de Valera
Irish Fairy Tales £1.25

From the land of pixies, fairies, witches and druids, twelve strange and
wonderful stories of sorcery and magical spells – from the evil fairy who could
take the form of any animal, to the giant who stole the king's crown . . .

More Irish Fairy Tales £1.25

Ten more strange and wonderful stories of magical spells and emerald trees,
of witches and mighty kings . . . from the land of pixies and fairies and the
strangest of sorceries.

Piccolo fiction you will enjoy

○ **The Travels of Oggy**	⎫ Ann Lawrence	95p
○ **Oggy and the Holiday**	⎭	90p
○ **Flight of the Doves**	Walter Macken	£1.25p
○ **The Yearling**	Marjorie Kinnan Rawlings	£1.95p
○ **How to Eat Fried Worms**	Thomas Rockwell	£1.25p
○ **101 Dalmatians**	Dodie Smith	£1.50p
○ **Quincy**	Tommy Steele	95p
○ **Tales of Little Grey Rabbit**	Alison Uttley	£1.50p
○ **Bottersnikes and Gumbles**	S. A. Wakefield	£1.50p
○ **CLUTZ**	Marilyn Wilkes	£1.25p
○ **The Fastest Gun Alive**	⎫ David Henry Wilson	95p
○ **Elephants Don't Sit on Cars**	⎭	£1.25p
○ **The Fairy Tale Omnibus**		£2.95p

All these books are available at your local bookshop or newsagent, or can be ordered direct from the publisher. Indicate the number of copies required and fill in the form below   12

....

Name_____
(Block letters please)

Address_____

_____

Send to CS Department, Pan Books Ltd,
PO Box 40, Basingstoke, Hants
Please enclose remittance to the value of the cover price plus:
35p for the first book plus 15p per copy for each additional book
ordered to a maximum charge of £1.25 to cover postage and
packing
Applicable only in the UK

While every effort is made to keep prices low, it is sometimes
necessary to increase prices at short notice. Pan Books reserve the
right to show on covers and charge new retail prices which may
differ from those advertised in the text or elsewhere